ADVENTURE
KINGDOM

Written By
STEVE FOXE

Illustrated By
PEDRO RODRIGUEZ

Colors By
SONIA MORUNO

Adventure Kingdom created by
Steve Foxe and Pedro Rodriguez

Andrews McMeel Publishing
a division of Andrews McMeel Universal
1130 Walnut Street, Kansas City, Missouri 64106

www.andrewsmcmeel.com

Epic! Creations, Inc.
702 Marshall Street, Suite 280
Redwood City, California 94063

www.getepic.com

21 22 23 24 25 SDB 10 9 8 7 6 5 4 3 2 1

Paperback ISBN: 978-1-5248-6982-3
Hardback ISBN: 978-1-5248-7078-2

Library of Congress Control Number: 2021934738

Design by Dan Nordskog

Made by:
King Yip (Dongguan) Printing & Packaging Factory Ltd.
Address and location of manufacturer:
Daning Administrative District, Humen Town
Dongguan Guangdong, China 523930
1st Printing — 6/28/21

TO THE GREATEST JEROME I KNOW.
THANKS FOR ALL THE MAGIC, DAD.
S. F.

TO GEMMA AND MAYA.
P. R.

ADVENTURE KINGDOM

CHAPTER 1
KEY TO THE KINGDOM

7

WOW. THIS PLACE IS STILL AMAZING...

NO RACCOONS HERE.

ONE OF THESE DAYS I'M GONNA GET YOU A FRESH COAT OF PAINT, WINNIE. I CAN'T FIX EVERYTHING, BUT I CAN FIX YOU.

I REMEMBER YOU...

11

DID WE LOSE IT?

I DON'T KNOW. I HOPE SO.

YO, CLARKSIDE07 SIGNING BACK ON--

WILL YOU STOP THAT? HE'S GOING TO SEE THE LIGHT!

GIVE THAT BACK!

CLARKSIDE07
FOLLOWING: 3,547
FOLLOWERS: 8

EIGHT FOLLOWERS...?

IT...TAKES TIME TO BUILD AN AUDIENCE, OKAY?

HEY, TWO MORE AND YOU'LL BE IN DOUBLE DIGITS.

I'M KAROLINE, BY THE WAY.

MY NAME'S--

CLARKSIDE07. I KNOW.

CLARK, FOR SHORT.

SORRY ABOUT THE WHOLE FOLLOWERS THING.

THAT'S OKAY. I WASN'T TOTALLY HONEST, EITHER.

MY FAMILY ISN'T JUST TAKING CARE OF THIS PLACE.

MY GRANDAD BUILT IT. NOW THAT HE'S GONE, WE'RE JUST WATCHING IT FALL APART.

IF YOU'RE THE GRAND JEROME'S FLESH AND BLOOD, THEN THIS BELONGS TO YOU.

SORRY, I DIDN'T REALIZE WHO YOU WAS, BEFORE.

NO WAY--A TALKING MONKEY...

I GOT A NAME, KID. IT'S EDDIE.

HEY HEY HEY, FOLLOW--

DON'T. EVEN. START.

I'M SORRY TO SAY THE GRAND JEROME, HE AIN'T COMING BACK. NOT UNLESS YOU HELP HIM.

WHAT DO YOU MEAN, "THE GRAND JEROME?" ARE YOU TALKING ABOUT MY GRANDAD?

YEAH, I AM.

"JEROME BARKER. BOY, PEOPLE ON YOUR WORLD LOVED HIM.

"BUT BACK ON MY WORLD, WELL...LOVE HIM OR HATE HIM, THE GRAND JEROME WAS THE GREATEST WIZARD THERE EVER WAS."

GRANDAD WASN'T A WIZARD! HE WAS A LITTLE KOOKY, MAYBE...

LOOK, I SEEN THE GRAND JEROME USE THIS COIN. IT'S DANGEROUS IN THE WRONG HANDS.

THAT'S WHY WE GOTTA PROTECT IT--

YOU GOTTA BE KIDDIN' ME! IT'S THE BLASTED KID CAVALRY!

YOU WANT 'DIS? COME GET IT, YA KNUCKLEHEADS!

OHMYGOSH!

THAT'S IT, NO MORE MISTER NICE PIG.

LOOK OUT!

25

HE'S GONE AND DONE IT, BOSS. THAT DOUBLE-CROSSING EDDIE MADE OFF WITH THE GRAND PAIN-IN-THE-BUTT'S GOLDEN COIN.

TOOK A COUPLE A' HUMAN BRATS THROUGH THE WISHING WELL, TOO.

BUT DON'T WORRY. WE'LL GET THE COIN BACK.

THEY GOT NO IDEA WOT'S WAITING FOR 'EM ON THE OTHER SIDE!

ADVENTURE KINGDOM

Join the magical parade on the

Carousel of
ADVENTURE

CHAPTER 2
FRIENDS AND FORTUNES

THE COIN IS ALSO A KEY...

IF YOU WANT TO HELP THE GRAND JEROME, WE AIN'T GOT TIME TO ARGUE...

HE'S YOUR GRANDFATHER. IT'S YOUR CHOICE...

WHERE...?

OH NO. THE TALKING MONKEY AND EVIL PIG-MAN AND MY GRANDAD BEING A WIZARD--

ALL REAL, YO! AND DON'T FORGET THE *MAGIC COIN.*

I PREFER EDDIE OVER "TALKING MONKEY," KID.

AT LEAST HOGSWALLOP DIDN'T HITCH A RIDE WITH US. HE'S STILL STUCK BACK IN *YOUR* WORLD.

WHICH MEANS WE'RE IN...

33

I DON'T NOW...THIS IS GIVING ME A JOR CREEPY VIBES.

MAYBE THIS FORTUNE-TELLER LADY CAN FIND THE GRAND JEROME FOR US!

I DON'T REMEMBER NO FORTUNE-TELLER FROM THE OLD DAYS, THOUGH.

GOOD. THAT MEANS SHE CAN'T BE MAD AT YOU.

LOOK, YOU DON'T KNOW THE HALF OF IT. THE IRON KING WAS A TYRANT-- BAD AS THEY COME. WHEN HE TOOK OVER, PALS TURNED ON PALS.

THE GRAND JEROME LOCKED HIM AWAY, BUT THAT DON'T MEAN ALL THE WOUNDS HEALED RIGHT.

HOW ABOUT THIS CLARKSIDE07 EXCLUSIVE? EVIL WIZARDS, SUPERHERO MAGICIANS, *AND* OTHER DIMENSIONS.

BUT DON'T WORRY, FOLLOWERS, BECAUSE YOUR BOY IS ON THE CASE--

CREEEAAAK!

AHH!

I THINK THE DOOR IS ON A MECHANIZED HINGE. PROBABLY A GIMMICK TO MAKE THE FORTUNE-TELLER SEEM MORE MYSTERIOUS.

MAYBE THIS PLACE ISN'T AS MAGICAL AS YOU THOUGHT...

IS SHE...SLEEPING?

I THINK SHE'S A ROBOT OR SOMETHING--AND SHE'S OUT OF BATTERIES.

KNOCK!
KNOCK!

EVEN IF SHE IS A ROBOT, IT'S RUDE TO KNOCK ON HER HEAD LIKE THAT.

WHAT? I'M JUST SEEING IF SHE HAS A HIDDEN SWITCH.

UGH. EDDIE, DO YOU KNOW HOW TO WAKE HER UP?

DON'T LOOK AT ME, KID. SHE'S GIVING ME THE CREEPS.

OH HEY, THERE'S A COIN SLOT! MAYBE THIS'LL WORK.

WAIT--IT COULD GET STUCK! WHAT IF WE NEED IT TO GET HOME AGAIN?

41

HELLO, LUNA. I'M--

WAIT, WHY DO *YOU* GET TO ASK?

HUSH, KID!

YOU'RE KAROLINE. YOU POSSESS A KIND HEART, AND YOU'RE SEARCHING FOR SOMEONE DEAR TO YOU.

SPiiiN!

SOMEONE WHO IS LOCKED AWAY, TRAPPED IN A HALL OF MIRRORS...OF HIS OWN MAKING.

HEY, YOU'RE GOOD! DO ME NEXT! AND DO YOU MIND IF I RECORD THIS?

CLARK!

OH CLARK. DO WE REALLY WANT TO SHARE THE TRUTH?

SUCH AN IMPORTANT DAY FOR YOU...MARKED BY SUCH A SAD ENDING. PARENTS ALWAYS ARGUING. PRETENDING IT WASN'T ABOUT YOU.

ENOUGH. JUST LEAVE US ALONE. WE DON'T NEED YOUR "HELP."

CLARK, CLARK. I KNOW THE TRUTH IS PAINFUL, BUT LET'S NOT DO ANYTHING WE'LL REGRET.

MAYBE YOU DON'T KNOW ME AS WELL AS YOU THINK! I'LL SHATTER THIS THING IN A HEARTBEAT.

CLARK, STARCHILD. YOU'RE IN *OUR* WORLD NOW. THERE ARE FORCES IN CONTROL HERE THAT NONE OF US CAN AFFORD TO UPSET.

YOU DON'T NEED THESE MAKE-BELIEVE FRIENDS OR THAT SILLY MAGIC TOKEN.

SET DOWN THE CRYSTAL BALL, AND GIVE ME THE *COIN!*

WOW, THESE RINGALINGS ARE AMAZING!

AND NO ONE HERE IS TRYING TO *RINGALING* MY NECK. BIG IMPROVEMENT OVER THE BOARDWALK!

TA-DAH!

I'LL ADMIT IT--THIS IS PRETTY COOL.

BUT WHERE'S THE AUDIENCE?

EDDIE, ALL THESE VILLAGERS LOOK... SCARED.

WELCOME TO LIFE UNDER THE IRON KING, KID. CAN'T EVEN ENJOY A SHOW WITHOUT WORRYING ABOUT WHO'LL CRASH IT.

ERR...DID YOU MENTION THE IRON KING?

YES! WE'RE LOOKING FOR THE GRAND JEROME, AND A--WELL, ACTUALLY A PRETTY EVIL ROBOT SAID WE COULD FIND HIM IN A HALL OF MIRRORS.

SHH! THE RINGALINGS DON'T PICK SIDES.

BUT YOUR AUDIENCE IS TERRIFIED! IF YOUR GOAL IS TO SPREAD JOY, THEN YOU HAVE TO STAND AGAINST THE IRON KING.

THIS SHOW'S NO GOOD. NO ONE HAS FALLEN OR BROKEN ANYTHING!

GO ON, MARBLES, SHOW 'EM WHAT YOU THINK.

HEHEHEHE!

SPLAT!

HA HA HA HA!

PLEASE, PLEASE, WE HAVE NO STAKE IN THIS WAR! TAKE THE CHILD'S COIN AND LEAVE US ALONE!

POP CORN

HEHEHE, IT REALLY IS YOU, EDDIE. IT'S BEEN A LONG TIME.

OH NO. ARE THESE MORE OF YOUR *OLD PALS,* EDDIE?

WE'RE THE ORGAN-GRINDERS. I'M ORVILLE. THESE LUNKHEADS ARE LENNIE AND MARBLES.

WE RIDE UNDER THE FLAG OF THE IRON KING. AND EDDIE HERE WAS OUR LITTLE SPY.

"HE WAS *SLIPPERY ENOUGH* TO TRICK THE GRAND JEROME INTO TRUSTING HIM. OUR *MONKEY ON THE INSIDE.*"

71

DOUBLE-CROSS, TRIPLE-CROSS! LITTLE EDDIE CAN'T KEEP HIS LOYALTIES STRAIGHT.

HEHEHEHEHE!

KAROLINE, WATCH OUT!

I DON'T KNOW IF I CAN *TRUST* YOU, EDDIE, BUT THIS TOWN AND THE RINGALINGS NEED US. AND SO DOES CLARK.

SO LET'S CALL A TRUCE FOR NOW. YOU CAN EXPLAIN LATER.

PLEASE, KID! I MAY HAVE STARTED AS A SPY, BUT I WAS LOYAL TO YOUR GRANDFATHER.

I'M NOT WITH THESE ZOO REJECTS. NOT ANYMORE.

THIS IS MY FAULT! I THOUGHT IF THEY TOOK YOUR MAGIC COIN, THEY'D LEAVE *US* ALONE.

WE ALL MAKE MISTAKES. WHAT MATTERS IS WHAT YOU DO *AFTERWARD*.

WHATEVER WE'RE GOING TO DO--UNHH--WE'D BETTER DO IT SOON. THOSE APES ARE STILL OUT THERE.

YOU WERE WILLING TO TURN OVER *CHILDREN?*

I'M SORRY. I WAS SCARED... I DIDN'T KNOW WHAT ELSE TO DO...

IF YOU GIVE ME A CHANCE, I CAN FIX THIS MESS.

AND THEN I CAN EXPLAIN *EVERYTHING.*

HERE'S YOUR COIN BACK.

IF YOU WANT, I CAN STAY BEHIND AND--

EDDIE...WE'RE *NOT* LEAVING WITHOUT YOU.

WE'LL ALL STAY AND HELP CLEAN UP, RIGHT CLARK?

I KINDA WANT TO THROW EDDIE IN THE CAGE TOO...BUT HE DID HELP SAVE US ALL BACK THERE.

IF YOU SAY THERE'S MORE TO YOUR STORY, YOU'VE EARNED A CHANCE TO TELL IT.

THEN WE'LL SHOW THIS TOWN A *REAL* RINGALING PRODUCTION.

AND TAKE *ALL THREE* OF YOU TO THE HALL OF MIRRORS. IT'S THE LEAST WE CAN DO.

WHERE ARE THESE GOONS GOING?

THE MIDDLE OF NOWHERE. LET THEM *WALK* BACK TO CIVILIZATION.

WHAT ABOUT MY STORY?

TELL IT WHILE WE WORK. THEN WE'LL *REALLY* GIVE YOU A CHANCE.

IT ALL STARTED WHEN I WAS JUST A BABY MONKEY...

Drive like a monkey at the

BARREL OF MONKEYS
Bumper Cars

ADVENTURE KINGDOM

THE IRON KING BUILT THIS PLACE, BUT THE GRAND JEROME BOOTED HIM OUT.

HOLD UP A SECOND, EDDIE.

WHATEVER WE FIND IN THERE WITH YOUR GRANDAD, I'LL BE RIGHT BY YOUR SIDE...

...AND SO WILL EDDIE.

CLARK'S RIGHT, BUT IF YOU TWO DON'T PUT SOME PEP IN YOUR STEP, I'M GOING TO BE IN THERE *ALONE.*

WE'RE COMING, WE'RE COMING. DON'T GET YOUR LITTLE MONKEY TAIL IN A TWIST.

I'M GLAD YOU AND CLARK ARE SUCH PALS, BUT DO YOU GOTTA SOUND LIKE HIM NOW, TOO?

89

MIMEO! C'MON OUT.

CRACK!

I WONDERED WHEN YOU'D SUMMON ME. I'VE BEEN *WATCHING*...

SEE, YOU SAYING STUFF LIKE THAT GIVES ME THE CREEPS. BUT THE IRON KING NEEDS YOUR, UH, *UNIQUE* SERVICES.

THERE'S THESE TWO BRATS, SEE, AND...

OOF!

MADE IT!

ALL RIGHT, EDDIE--TIME TO MONKEY UP!

EDDIE!

AND YOU, YOUNG MAN—I'M TERRIBLE AT NAMES. I WANT TO SAY, ERR...CALDWELL? CALEB? CARTER?

IT COULDN'T POSSIBLY BE... CLARK!

I, UH, KEPT YOUR COIN SAFE FOR YOU. MOSTLY.

YOU'VE DONE MUCH MORE THAN THAT, CLARK.

AND IT'S NOT *MY* COIN. NOT ANYMORE.

LET'S CONTINUE THIS REUNION BACK IN MY QUARTERS, THOUGH. ALL THIS DUST IS CLOGGING MY MUSTACHE!

WHOA, MAGIC DOOR!

CRACK!

CLARK...YOU *DO* KNOW WE HAVE HIDDEN DOORS IN THE REAL WORLD, RIGHT?

BUT...YOU DIDN'T EVEN KNOW WHO I WAS WHEN YOU GAVE ME MY PIECE.

I RECOGNIZED THE GLINT OF WONDER IN YOUR EYE AND TRUSTED FATE TO BE RIGHT.

AND KAROLINE, YOU'VE IMPRESSED ME SINCE THE DAY YOU WERE BORN.

SO, WITH YOUR MAGIC COIN, WON'T YOU BE STRONG ENOUGH TO BEAT THE IRON KING AGAIN?

AH, THE COIN IS A KEY, NOT A WEAPON. BUT I DIDN'T BEAT THE IRON KING BY BEING STRONGER THAN HIM-- I DID IT BY BRINGING ADVENTURE KINGDOM *TOGETHER*.

"I WASN'T SURE I COULD DO THAT A SECOND TIME, BUT I HAD A FEELING YOU KIDS COULD. AND SEEING YOU HERE NOW MEANS THAT FEELING WAS CORRECT.

"BUT ALL OF THE **GRAND JEROME** STUFF IS JUST AN...INSPIRING MYTH.

"AND WHEN I CAME BACK HERE, I REALIZED THAT NO MYTH COULD COMPETE WITH FEAR OF THE IRON KING."

GRANDAD, YOU'RE MORE THAN A MYTH. I ALWAYS TRY TO DO WHAT'S RIGHT BECAUSE OF YOU. THE PARK YOU BUILT INSPIRED CLARK. EDDIE DEFECTED FROM THE IRON KING TO JOIN YOU!

YEAH! WE KEPT THIS SAFE JUST FOR YOU! PLENTY OF **MAJOR** BAD GUYS HAVE BEEN TRYING TO STEAL--

CRACK!

--THIS COIN!

SNAP!

WHAT THE... HEY, LET GO!

MIMEO! ONE OF THE IRON KING'S SNEAKIEST SPIES. IT CAN TRAVEL THROUGH MIRRORS--DON'T LET IT PULL YOU IN!

PULL M-- *WHOA!*

CLARK!

WE GOTTA GET HIM BACK! USE YOUR MAGIC!

I'D GIVE ANYTHING TO DO SO, EDDIE. BUT I CAN'T ACCESS MIMEO'S REALM.

I *CAN* OPEN A GATEWAY BACK TO THE THEME PARK, WHERE MIMEO IS LIKELY TAKING CLARK-- BUT IT WILL REQUIRE ALL OF MY FOCUS TO *HOLD* IT OPEN.

CONFRONTING THE IRON KING WILL BE UP TO YOU TWO ALONE.

CHAPTER 5
THE GRAND FINALE

122

126

EDDIE, KEEP THE OTHERS ORGANIZED.

WE NEED THE IRON KING'S FORCES *OUT* OF THE WAY.

AYE-AYE, CAPTAIN!

WE NEED TO GET THAT COIN BACK BEFORE HE THROWS IT INTO THE WISHING WELL.

AND SINCE HE'S GOT A DRAGON, WE NEED RIDES OF OUR OWN.

ACTUALLY, THERE'S A TRICK I SAW IN AN OLD MOVIE ONCE...

SORRY, THERE'S **NO WAY** I'M LETTING YOU TOUCH THIS AGAIN.

YOUR REIGN OF TERROR IS OVER FOR GOOD.

YEAH, WHAT SHE SAID.

SO, JEROME'S GRANDDAUGHTER WANTS TO FINISH WHAT HE STARTED. HOW **USELESS.**

THERE'S NO PRISON TO HOLD ME NOW. YOUR FAMILY'S PARK IS IN SHAMBLES!

BESIDES, I STILL HAVE **THE COIN!** AS LONG AS I CONTROL ITS MAGIC, I'LL NEVER--

THAT'S RIGHT. AND THERE'S ENOUGH MAGIC LEFT IN THE COIN FOR ONE LAST WISH.

WHOOSH!

BUH-BYE!

YOU DIDN'T LIKE PRISON. LET'S SEE HOW YOU ENJOY *EXILE.*

YOU CAN'T DO THIS TO ME. I CAN'T FAIL AGAIN. I--

I HOPED YOU THREE WOULD SUCCEED.

AND HOPE IS POWERFUL MAGIC!

THE IRON KING WAS RIGHT ABOUT ONE THING, THOUGH--THE PARK LOOKS WORSE THAN *EVER*.

BUT WITHOUT THE COIN, HOW DO WE GET EVERYONE HOME?

WE WON'T GIVE UP UNTIL WE FIND A WAY. I PROMISE.

IN THE MEANTIME, I DO HAVE ONE *OTHER* IDEA...

ABOUT THE AUTHOR

STEVE FOXE is the author of more than fifty comics and children's books for properties including *Pokémon*, *Batman*, *Adventure Time*, *Steven Universe*, *Far Out Fables*, and *Spider-Ham*, as well as quite a few stories for adults. He lives in Queens with his partner and dog, but he visits theme parks every chance he gets.

ABOUT THE ILLUSTRATOR

PEDRO RODRIGUEZ studied illustration at the Fine Arts School La Llotja in Barcelona, Spain. He has worked on a variety of projects in design, marketing, advertising, publishing, animated films, and music videos. He has illustrated more than forty books and comic books. Pedro lives next to the beach, close to Barcelona, with his wife, Gemma, and their daughter, Maya.

The Characters of
ADVENTURE KINGDOM

KAROLINE

Adventure Kingdom runs in Karoline's blood. No, really--her grandad founded the theme park. Karoline knows how to shoulder responsibility, but in Adventure Kingdom she learns to let down her defenses and make friends, too.

CLARK

Don't let Clark's anything-goes persona fool you--while it seems like he treats everything like a joke, he'll do whatever it takes to protect his friends...as long as he can livestream it for his followers at the same time.

EDDIE

Whoa, a talking monkey! Eddie seems to know everyone in and everything about the real Adventure Kingdom... but his new friends may not know everything about him.

THE GRAND JEROME

The Grand Jerome had a vision for the most awe-inspiring theme park in all the land, and then he turned that vision into reality--using a genuine magic touch.

HOGSWALLOP

When the wicked Iron King first marched across the magical land of Adventure Kingdom, a few of its residents willingly joined his side, starting with this porcine terror. Hogswallop is a goon through and through, and he'll do whatever it takes to restore his master to power.

BEHIND THE SCENES

Epic makes comics by bringing together the best writers and artists to collaborate on stories filled with action, humor, and heart. But that process takes time and work!

1. SCRIPT

The first step in creating any comic book is for the writer to come up with the plot and dialogue. Here's Steve Foxe talking about his process for *Adventure Kingdom*.

"One of the great things about a long-term creative relationship is learning more about your collaborator as you go along. For instance, I learned pretty early on that Pedro has a great sense of pacing, so I don't have to get too specific about how panels should be placed on the page. Pedro is also really skilled at depicting nuanced emotions, so I don't have to spell out how a character is feeling in the dialogue--he handles it right on their faces."

Page 3

Panel 1:
Soon after, Eddie crests up from a dip in the path and points into the near distance. Clark and Karoline both have concerned looks on their face.

1 EDDIE: Sorry kiddo, but your grandfather is kind of a legend in my world. The Iron King never could compete.

2 EDDIE: But why am I flapping my gums? We're here!

3 EDDIE: Bright-Sky Boardwalk! Our premiere seaside destination.

Panel 2:
Bigger panel as we see Bright-Sky Boardwalk, which is much gloomier than the name portends. Think classic early 20th-century boardwalks, now weathered and cast under never-ending grey skies. As for residents, let's at least stick to folks who look like they're in old-timey bathing suits or sailor suits, to stay on theme? In one corner of the shot, we should see SLAPPY the sea lion, dozing next to a half-deflated balancing ball. Slappy has smeared clown paint on, a hat, and maybe a neck ruffle too? The other thing we should definitely see, and potentially a few times around these scenes, is a balloon stand or cart with lots of balloons tied to it.

NO DIALOGUE

Panel 3:
Close on Karoline and Clark grimacing at each other.

4 CLARK: More like "Mostly Cloudy Boardwalk"...

5 KAROLINE: Yeah, is this the best this place has to offer, Eddie?

Panel 4:
Eddie, possessing of some wounded pride (and maybe a little guilt), stands up for the Boardwalk.

6 EDDIE: Ya don't have to be rude about it. I told you Adventure Kingdom has seen better days. But it'll all get fixed once we find the Grand Jerome.

7 EDDIE: Like I said, I know a gu--

8 SLAPPY [off-panel]: Eddie! Eddie, you rotten rat-monkey, is that you?

2. ROUGH PENCILS

Every artist has their own process, but here's how Pedro approaches each issue of *Adventure Kingdom*.

"After several readings of Steve's script, I make a first quick sketch in order to fit the scenes into panels. After that, I make another, more defined sketch according to what the script asks for."

3. INKS

After the sketches are approved by the author and the editor, the artist turns them into final, inked drawings. Drawings will often change in response to feedback from Steve and Epic's team of editors and designers.

"When inking, I make small changes that would improve upon the sketch. I also work on additional details, as well as facial expressions."

4. COLOR

Next comes the color. For *Adventure Kingdom*, Pedro works with colorist Sonia Moruno to give the world more life and depth.

"With the color, the atmosphere is created, and we look for the drama needed in each scene. Now is the moment to find the lights and shadows in every panel."

HAVE YOU HEARD ABOUT epic! YET?

We're the largest digital library for kids, used by millions in homes and schools around the world. We love stories so much that we're now creating our own!

With the help of some of the best writers and illustrators in the world, we create the wildest adventures we can think of. Like a mermaid and a narwhal who solve mysteries. Or a pet made out of slime.

We hope you have as much fun reading our books as we had making them!

LOOK FOR THESE BOOKS FROM

epic!

AVAILABLE **NOW!**

TO READ MORE, VISIT
getepic.com